WALT DISNEY PRODUCTIONS
presents

Sindbad the Pearl Diver

Random House 🏠 **New York**

Sindbad the sailor was home from the sea.
He was eager to see his friend Minnie.
Her father was a rich ship owner.

Sindbad set off for Minnie's house.
On the way he met two strangers.
"We want to talk to you!" the men said.

Sindbad wondered what the men wanted.
"Come have lunch with us and
we'll explain," said the men.
So Sindbad did a very foolish thing.
He went off with the strangers!

The men took Sindbad to a restaurant.
"Let's have something to eat here,"
said one of the men. "Waiter!"

But the waiter did not bring food.

He tied a napkin around Sindbad's face instead!

Sindbad could not even cry for help.

Something in the napkin made Sindbad
fall asleep quickly.

When night came, the two strange men
carried Sindbad onto the ship MINNIE.

The men took Sindbad below deck
and left him there.

Back on deck the men laughed.
"We have enough divers now!"
said the captain of the ship.
"We'll set sail in the morning."

"All hands on deck!" called the captain
early the next day. "Heave ho!"
The crew hauled on the ropes.

Up went the sails.

The ship sailed out of the harbor.

Minnie's father owned the ship MINNIE.

But Sindbad did not know that.

Sindbad was still sleeping in the hold.
One of the crew came to wake him up.
"Time to start work!" the man snarled.

Other captives were in the hold too.
The sailor ordered them all up on deck.
"Hurry up!" the man said to them.

"Get ready
for diving!"
the captain sai
"Into the boats

Sindbad and another captive were put
into a small boat with a sailor.

The boat was lowered into the sea.

Away they went over the waves.

The sailor stopped rowing after a while.
Nearby, men were diving for oysters.
"In you go!" roared the sailor. "And
make sure you come up with pearl oysters!"

So Sindbad took a deep breath
and dived into the water.

Sindbad swam down and down.
He filled his net bag with oysters.
He had to dive again and again.

By sunset the small boats
were filled with oyster shells.
Then the boats returned
to the ship MINNIE.

The captain and his mate
looked at the shells.

"Not bad for beginners,"
sneered the captain.

But there was still more work to be done that night.

The captives had to look for pearls
in the oyster shells.

The pearls went into the mate's sack.

Finally the sun began to rise.
Sindbad and the other prisoners went
into the hold to get some sleep.

"We'll be rich men after this voyage!"
the captain said to his mate. "Let's tell
the owner of the ship MINNIE that a storm
came up. We'll say we didn't find any
pearls. We'll keep them all for us!"

Then they steered the ship MINNIE
toward the home port.

Back at home
Sindbad's friend
Minnie was worried

Sindbad's ship had arrived in port.
But Sindbad had disappeared!
Minnie's father was worried too.
He had lost one ship at sea.
His ship MINNIE was late.
And he owed money to many people.

There was
a loud knock
at the door.
"Maybe
that is
Sindbad!"
said Minnie.

Three men were at the door.
Minnie's father owed them money.

"We cannot wait forever!" the men said
to Minnie's father. "We must be paid
now—or we will take your home from you!"
  "But my home is all I have left!"
cried Minnie's father.

Then the group heard "Ship ahoy!"
They all ran down to the harbor.
The ship MINNIE was coming into port!

Minnie, her father, and the other men
boarded the ship.

The captives watched from the hold.

"Good news?" asked Minnie's father.
"We had bad luck," lied the captain.
"We didn't find any pearl oysters, sir."
"I am ruined!" said the ship's owner.
The captives had heard everything.

The prisoners broke out of the hold and ran up on deck.

"We'll tell you what really happened!" Sindbad said to Minnie's father.

The ship owner
heard the true story.

The captain
and his mate
were tied up
and taken off
the ship.

"I know where
the pearls are,"
Sindbad said
to Minnie and
her father.
"I'm so glad
you're safe!"
Minnie said.

Sindbad handed
the sack of pearls
to its real owner.
"You have saved
my home, Sindbad!"
said Minnie's father.

"At last I can pay my debts!"
the happy ship owner said.

He gave the pearls to the men
to whom he owed money.

"You are a hero, Sindbad!" Minnie said.

Soon the ship MINNIE
was ready to sail again.
And the new captain
in command was Sindbad!